Tonka®

WORKING HARD WITH THE MIGHTY CRANE™

Written by Justine Korman
Illustrated by Steven James Petruccio

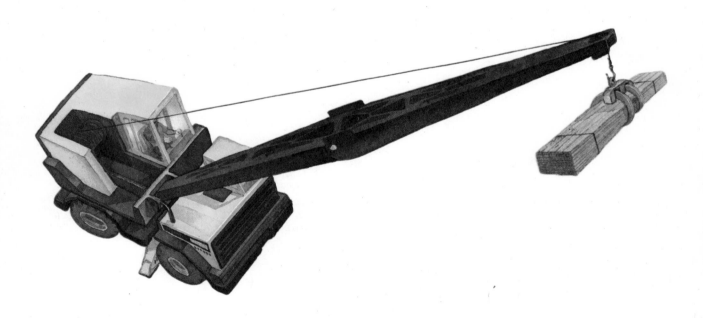

SCHOLASTIC INC.
New York Toronto London Auckland Sydney

ISBN 0-590-13094-3

TONKA® and TONKA® logo are trademarks of Hasbro, Inc.
Used with permission.
Copyright © 1998 by Hasbro, Inc. All rights reserved.
Published by Scholastic Inc.

12 11 10 9 8 7 6 5 4 3 2 1   8 9/9 0/0 01 02

Printed in the U.S.A.   24
First printing, May 1998

Lou gets up just before the sun so he can go fishing before work. Lou loves his job. He drives and operates a truck crane.

Lou's fishing pole reminds him of the truck crane's long arm. A crane is a machine that lifts heavy objects with a long, movable arm.

Lou hooks a big fish! He reels it in. The fishing line is like the cables on Lou's crane. By making the cables shorter, Lou pulls in a load — just like he reels in the fish.

Lou isn't alone at the lake. There's a hungry crane craning its neck to pull weeds from the water. A crane is a bird with a very long neck, like the arm of Lou's truck crane. To crane means to stretch.

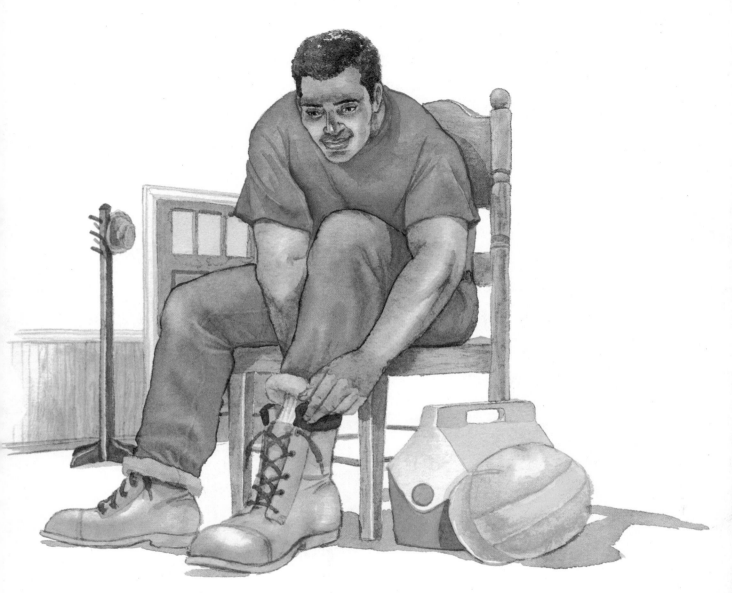

Back at home, Lou puts on his work gear. Like other construction workers, Lou wears steel-toed boots to protect his feet from falling objects. He also wears a bright yellow hard hat.

On the way to work, Lou sees a crawler crane lifting pipes in a marsh. The crawler crane lifts things just like Lou's truck crane.

But it moves on long, wide tracks instead of tires.
The tracks work like snowshoes to spread out the
crane's weight so it won't sink in soft ground.

Lou used to drive a crawler crane. But he likes his truck crane even better. Truck cranes don't need to ride on another truck to get to work!

Lou arrives at the construction site. It looks like a big, messy sand pile today. But after many hardworking months, there will be a giant office tower, a parking garage, storage sheds, and other small buildings.

First, Lou talks to the foreman. The foreman is the boss of the construction site. He tells all the workers what to do each day. The foreman holds plans drawn by an architect.

Architects decide what the building will look like. They make sure it will do what it's supposed to do, and that it has windows, plumbing, and electricity in all the right places.

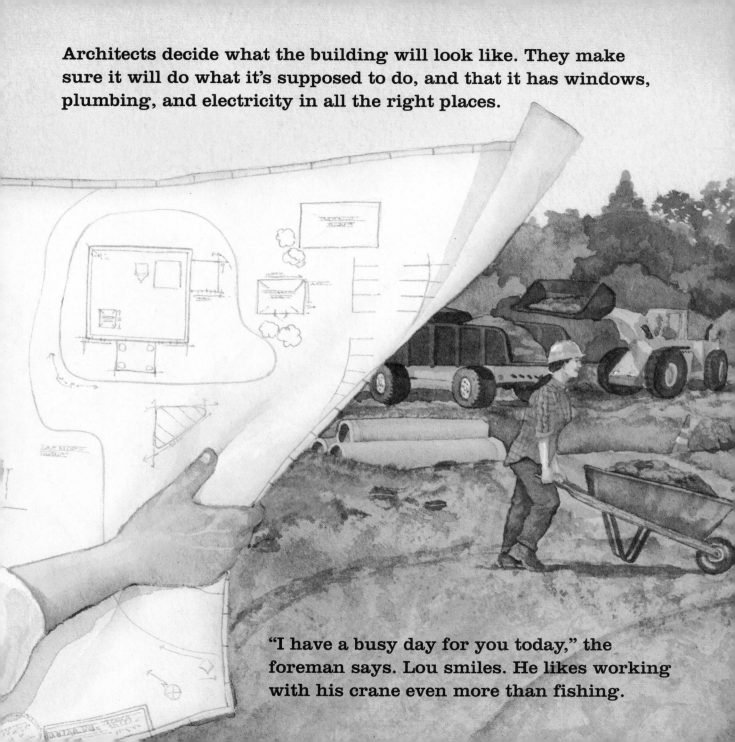

"I have a busy day for you today," the foreman says. Lou smiles. He likes working with his crane even more than fishing.

The first step of any truck crane job is to get in position and set up the outriggers. Outriggers are special legs that hold the truck crane steady, even while it's lifting very heavy loads. They also take the weight off the truck's tires.

The biggest truck cranes can lift about 1,000 tons!
Lou's crane isn't that big, but he wouldn't want a huge
load pressing down on the truck's wheels.

Lou doesn't work alone with his truck crane. Dan is a rigger. Thanks to different riggings, Lou's truck crane can do many different jobs. Right now, he wants it to be a digging machine. So Dan helps Lou attach the clamshell bucket.

Dan stands outside the truck to help Lou decide which way to move the crane's arm. Lou can also make the arm longer, like a crane stretching out its neck.

Dan uses his hands and arms to signal to Lou in the truck crane's cab. When they were children, Lou and Dan played baseball together. Lou was the pitcher and Dan was the catcher.

The hand signals they use today serve the same purpose as the ones they used during baseball games: to communicate across a distance without using words. The busy construction site is too noisy for words to be heard!

After the ditch is dug, Lou and Dan move on to their
next job. Once the outriggers are in place, they take off
the clamshell and attach the electromagnet.

The magnet is used to lift metal, like steel beams, for building frames. Moving the heavy beams is a tricky job.

After lunch, Lou uses his truck crane to load gravel. He and Dan attach the dragline rig. Lou works the controls in the truck's cab to move the cables attached to the bucket. The cables pull the bucket of gravel along the crane's arm.

Dan signals for Lou to move the load a little to the left. Then with a loud CLATTER the bucket empties into the bed of a dump truck.

With the tined grapple, Lou's truck crane can lift lumber for the carpenters. Tines are sharp points, like the prongs of a fork.

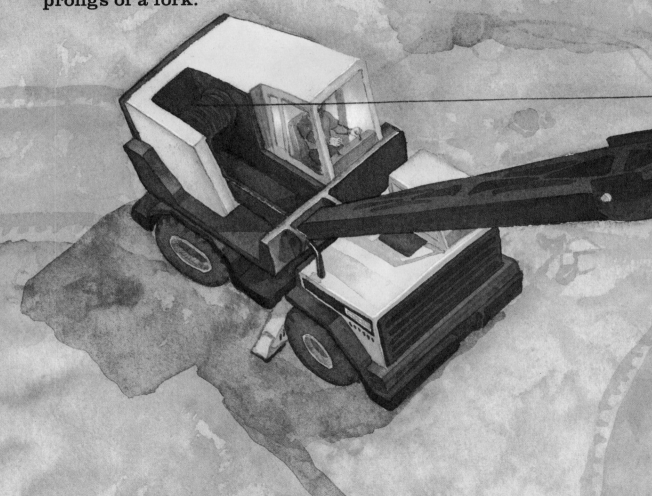

On big farms, people use tined grapples to move bales of hay. The tines look like giant metal fingers.

The last job of the day is the most exciting. Lou's truck crane gets to help build another crane!

Tower cranes are the tallest cranes. They are used to build skyscrapers and other things that require materials to be lifted way up high.

Most tower cranes are too big to travel.
So they are built right on the construction site! Lou's
crane places a cab on top of the tower crane's base.

Now the tower crane will build itself by adding one section of frame at a time. The crane will grow along with the building it helps to build.

After work, Lou, Dan, and their friends go bowling. Lou lifts the heavy ball with his arm and looks down the long lane. He imagines his crane rigged with its wrecking ball.

"A little to the left," Dan cautions.

Lou rolls the ball. It knocks down all the pins! Lou's friends whoop like whooping cranes.

On the way home, Lou sees a crane flying. He wonders if it is also going home to rest before another busy day.